THE
FOUR SEASONS
OF
BRAMBLY
HEDGE

JILL BARKLEM

TED SMART

CONTENTS

THIS EDITION PRODUCED FOR
THE BOOK PEOPLE LTD,
GUARDIAN HOUSE, BOROUGH ROAD,
GODALMING, SURREY GU7 2AE

© THIS EDITION JILL BARKLEM 1988
© TEXT AND ILLUSTRATIONS
SPRING STORY, SUMMER STORY
AUTUMN STORY, WINTER STORY
JILL BARKLEM 1980
NINTH IMPRESSION 1997

ISBN 0 583 32638-2

PRINTED IN ITALY

A
C O N V E R S A T I O N
W I T H
J I L L   B A R K L E M

In 1980 Collins published four little picture books by a young author and illustrator, Jill Barklem. SPRING STORY, SUMMER STORY, AUTUMN STORY and WINTER STORY chronicle in astonishing illustrative detail the lives and adventures of a community of mice who live in Brambly Hedge, a safe and idyllic spot where old values flourish and self-sufficiency is the order of the day.

Intended for small children, the books were an immediate success with readers of all ages and in a short time the Brambly Hedge stories had been translated into thirteen languages and over a million copies had been sold.

3

Very much in the English nursery tradition, the books nevertheless have their own identity, and eight years later, in spite of imitators, the Brambly Hedge mice continue to attract new admirers. How is it that Jill Barklem has evoked such an affectionate and loyal response from her readers? And what is it that is so remarkable about the world she portrays? The best person to provide the answers to these and the many other questions raised by the books is the author herself, and perhaps we should start at the beginning.

I was born in Epping and I have lived in or near it ever since. My father owns a department store, one of the old fashioned kind. He comes from a long line of London drapers. My mother is from an old Essex family. My grandfather was gardener in a big house near Epping, and through my mother, I think I have been greatly influenced by him. My great-grandfather was an hostler. He had an inn in a small hamlet called Thrushes Bush. My great-grandmother was rather like Mrs. Apple in character – she used to supply local old people with hams and cheeses and pickled

4

walnuts, as well as helping my great-grandfather in the inn.

I have one sister, three years older than myself. Our childhood was quiet and in most ways uneventful. My parents both have strong Christian convictions and their belief is of a practical kind which permeated our family life.

I always enjoyed being close to nature and one of my favourite pastimes was to retire to a patch of wild grass under a chestnut tree at the end of our garden where I used to observe the busy lives of tiny red spiders as they sped about in and out of the stems; concoct bluebell glue, make scent from rose petals and play house with my cloth doll Joan. I liked to draw and paint there too.

When I was thirteen, I suffered a detached retina and this played a key role in my development. Overnight it seemed, I changed from being a normal active child to a much more isolated, introspective one. I was no longer able to take part in any sport and so at school I could choose the sanctuary of the library or the artroom. I mainly chose the latter and spent

5

hours drawing twigs and skulls, flowers and leaves.

When it was time to make a choice about my future, I hesitated between zoology and art. It was a difficult decision because I had excellent teachers for both subjects and both encouraged me. In the end I applied to St Martin's School of Art in London where I was accepted to study illustration. I did not have a very clear idea of my future but assumed I would earn my living illustrating other people's books. I certainly never imagined that one day I would write my own.

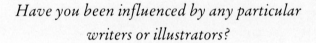

Have you been influenced by any particular writers or illustrators?

Although I don't come from a bookish family, I used to read an enormous amount as a child and as a teenager, particularly after my operation. I loved

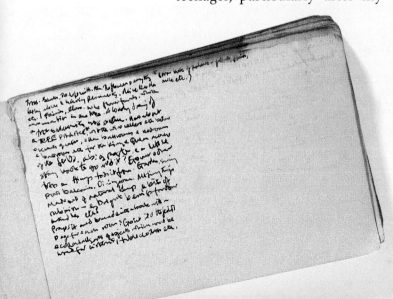

YARROW
Achillea Millefolium.
Family - Compositae - daisy.

Fitter & Blamey 238. Short/medium perennial, downy, aromatic. Lvs 2-3 pinnate feathery, dark green
Flheads short rayed, rays white or pink. disc florets creamy, in flat, umbel-like clusters. June-Nov.
Creamy stalks.

Keble Martin - 45 - Stoloniferous.

Englishman's Flora 403. also called 'Bunch o daisies' 'angel flower' 'morning evening' etc.
A wound herb. also against evil. — a woman's incantation for picking yarrow —
'I will pick the smooth yarrow that my figure may be sweeter, that my lips may be
warmer, that my voice may be gladder. May my voice be like a sunbeam, may my
lips be like the juice of the strawberry. May I be an island in the sea, may I be
a hill in the land, may I be a star in the dark time, may I be a staff to the weak one:
I shall wound every man, and no man shall hurt me'
If you put it up your nose it will make it bleed if you love loves you'

Food for Free 87. Pl. 3. Used in small quantities can make a cool, if rather bitter
addition to salads. Can be used as a green vegetable by removing the feathery leaves,
from the tough stems, boiling for 20 minutes. Straining of water, & simmering in butter.

Culpepers Herbal 398. Oval seed. Leaves dried & powdered, & put up nose, good for
sneezing & getting rid of 'inveterate headaches'
Has good astringent properties.

Felix & Toman 158
Frs For All 121
Used as wound healing, blood staunching
herb.
While yarrow plant in feet made
a good morning foot bath
A bitter herb — cows grazed on it make
bitter butter.
Yarrow tea — to sweat out a cold, or
as a digestive tonic.
Yarrow ointment (boiled in lard till
the fat goes green, then cooled) supposed
to cure baldness.

Clogwyn - Tresaman - Merionett — Sept 75
This was growing by the door of the cottage - indeed
all over the garden - but I picked this one by the door.
We were going to have some for supper one night,
but never got round to it

books. I loved the smell of them, the feel of the binding, the magical way they transported me away from everyday life. As a small child, I used to enjoy the Little Grey Rabbit books, *The Lion, the Witch and the Wardrobe* by C. S. Lewis, the Milly-Molly-Mandy stories, The Flower Fairies and everything Enid Blyton ever wrote. I didn't come across Winnie the Pooh or Beatrix Potter until much later when I was at art school. I liked non-fiction too, encyclopedias, atlases; *The Big Book of Engineering Feats* with its sepia reproductions of great achievements was a particular favourite.

I think I was most influenced by Arthur Rackham and by Leonardo da Vinci. I discovered him when I was at school and read everything I could find by him and about him. Arthur Ransome means a lot to me because of the Lake District setting and I read and reread Tolkien and Middlemarch.

wood mouse
'Mammals' Collins
Colour Guides.

Slightly too red —
should be yellower at
edges of colour.
115

Yellow necked field mouse
Mammals Collins.
118.

Striped field mouse
Central Europe.

common vole
very young.

Bank Vole.
103

*When did you develop the idea
of Brambly Hedge?*

I used to travel from Epping to London every day by
tube and I came to hate this journey. The carriages

Weaving.   July 7th 75.
I have just bought on a ghastly attack
of hay fever trying to weave a little
mat — but it was worth it! The first
week's ago (which I also bought
on hay fever!) didn't really
work very well. I started with
several grasses in a sort of
pile — like spokes in a wheel —

Then I tried to weave a
single grass round them.
This was very complicated —
e hard to handle — e the
thing kept going loose
e missing, but when it
got a bit bigger it was
better. Anyway — the thing
was fairly dreadful, e
ended up as a little basket
with a handle — but not
very organised at all —
e I have since lost it.
However today I went
about it in a more organised
way, e have made a small
mat out of two rushes

were crammed full of people; the trains, the tunnels, the stations, everything seemed so filthy. It was like a glimpse of hell. I dealt with it by shutting myself off completely and escaping into an inner world, a hedge bank of mice. They were nameless at that point, but I became obsessed with their way of life. I researched endlessly because it was important to me that every facet of it was accurate. I started to keep notebooks and diaries but it was essentially a private fantasy. It did not occur to me to show these to anyone at college.

I have recently realised that this inner world was one I began to explore much earlier — during the Sunday sermons when I was still a small child. I used to imagine a huge building, rather like a gymnasium. Half of it was taken up with a wooden construction full of little tunnels. These tunnels led to small rooms crammed full of interesting things. In my imagination, I used to crawl up the tunnels and examine all the treasures, each time finding something new and unexpected. The tunnels led up and up, finishing in a glass cupola. You could see for miles from there and it was always delightfully warm and cosy.

rushes with blackly
browny roots —
each slightly larger
the next — the one
e the brown one
messy, more papery.
very beautiful —
actually.
about 4ft
Capel Mead Drive
13/7/75.

11

It was also possible to go down the tunnels. At the bottom of some of them, you'd come upon the beginning of a long, curved slide, rather like a helter-skelter, and the journey down was an exciting one. I was completely and happily immersed in this imaginary world and it was quite disconcerting when the sermon was over and I had to return to the real one.

Does this mean that Brambly Hedge
is not based on any real place?

Brambly Hedge is totally real in the way a vision or a daydream is real. It is as if it has always existed and I have had the good fortune to discover it. I suppose it is a combination of my own fantasies and real places. There is for example a hedge in Epping Forest that gives visual reality to the fantasy but the landscape surrounding Brambly Hedge is also formed from parts of the Lake District, a place I feel deeply for and where I often stay. I am married now and have two

young children and so cannot retreat to the parallel reality of the Hedge at will, as I once used to do. I have to use a mental discipline to return to it but when I arrive, there it is, consistent and real just as I remember it.

Is the life the mice lead really feasible?

Yes, it is, apart from the occasional problem of scale. On a practical level, their clothes, food, housing and utensils are all provided by the Hedge or the surrounding countryside. The dairy, the flour mill, the looms are all fully functional, and run on water power or are paw operated.

Socially, the mice live in harmony with their environment and with each other. There is a philosophy of loving kindness and mutual responsibility. For example, Lord Woodmouse, who is nominal head of the community, lives in Old Oak Palace. His house is in the largest and oldest tree in the Hedge so he has both the responsibility of looking after it and of sharing it with the rest of the mice, for all the great events of the year are celebrated there. His role does

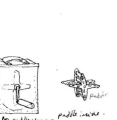

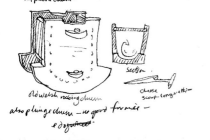

Elderflower Fritters
gather some fresh elderflowers

Make a batter from a small bowl of flour,
an egg, and enough water to make
a batter. Dip the flowers into batter
and fry in oil til golden. These are
Delicious!"

not make him more important than his fellow mice but does mean that his contribution has to be greater. Each privilege brings its responsibilities, each deprivation has its advantage in Brambly Hedge.

The details of their lives have much in common with early agricultural communities in this country: the harnessing of wind and water power, the imaginative use of natural ingredients, the preserving of the fruits of autumn for winter use, the ceremonies and celebrations that mark the turning points of the year.

The mice clearly enjoy preparing and eating food.
Is this something you share with them?

I *am* very interested in food. It is an ancient preoccupation – something we have in common with primitive man, and I'm fascinated by the way it has developed into an art. I collect cookery books and

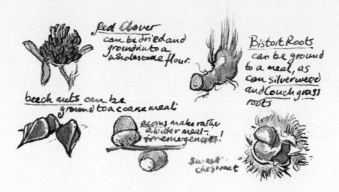

Red Clover
can be dried and
ground into a
wholesome flour.

Bistort Roots
can be ground
to a meal, as
can silverweed
and couch grass
roots

beech nuts can be
ground to a coarse meal

acorns make rather
a bitter meal –
for emergencies!

sweet
chestnut

over the years have built up a great deal of reference on old cooking practices. I like to put old ways of doing things to the test. The results can be delicious, though not in every case!

The social aspect of food is important to me too. Preparing food is an underestimated way of cherishing and showing love, a very simple yet very important domestic ritual.

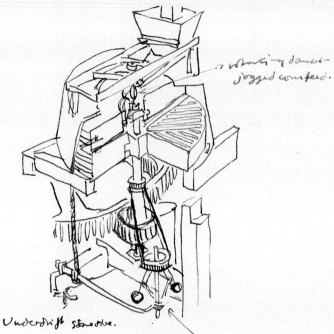

*How long does it take you to write
and illustrate a book?*

It usually takes me at least two years to produce a
book. First of all I do a great deal of research and
collect as much pictorial reference as I will need. I have

nut pinion –
3 removable teeth
to disengage it
from spur wheel.

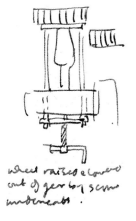

wheel raised a lowers
out of gear by screw
underneath.

piles of photographs in my workroom that I take with my Pentax and since I generally know what I'll want to draw, I am able to photograph suitable material when I come upon it. Also most of my books take place in a specific season and so it is important to take as many photographs as I can at the correct time.

Once I have completed the text, which will still be in draft form at this stage, I make a rough layout of all the pages, then I start on the detailed roughs for the individual pictures. I can do up to eighty rough drawings before I am satisfied with the composition and perspective. When I am ready to begin the finished illustration, I trace out my final rough onto a piece of Bristol board. Then I draw it out properly in pencil, checking for the last time that all the details are correct. Next I draw it out in sepia ink, putting in a blue wash for the shadow areas and a yellow one for sunlight, and slowly begin to build up the painting. A large illustration will take about three months.

I use, much to the consternation of my publisher and printer, cheaper water colours than most illustrators because I find that the result is softer and

somehow denser. I have a favourite nib – I'm always very anxious about losing or damaging it – and try to work for at least three hours at a stretch when I am drawing or painting. I like the company of the radio and can listen to talks and stories without losing my concentration but find it impossible to listen to music. It is too emotionally demanding.

Do you have any rituals to help you work?

I like to be surrounded by familiar possessions. Although we have moved house three times since I first started working on the Brambly Hedge books, my workroom, or more particularly my desk, remains exactly the same. The set of open drawers in which I store all my personal treasures has always been carefully packed and each item put back in the proper place in the new room.

Are these too traditional?

What materials will they make from?

Wool. Nettle. Flax.

Bleach with Arrowroot, & dye with all manner of roots, shoots, & fruits

Leather? Colours muted & soft

Weaving - done by the weavers. Like - made Arms from flax & nettle thread possibly very finely
spun wool. Weavers in own trees equipped with looms & spindles etc.

Fastenings - buttons - wood. Toggles. Wooden string hooks & eyes.

Wooden press studs. with expansion slits - but quite hard.

Clothes needed for protection ie aprons.

Mr Apple - working clothes - Tough apron? Willow
This wide.

I think hats look silly on animals.

Bonnets on sweet things, & mob caps.

Jackets rather obsolete.
Shirts, waistcoats,
aprons, dresses
look better. Coats
would probably be
full - not fitted

on the shirts -
wood buttons

Before beginning work, I exercise for ten minutes, finishing up in the fresh air no matter what the weather is like, and I also do eye exercises because the amount of close work I do strains them. Then I have a hot drink. I find it almost impossible to work in any room other than my own though if I'm travelling I can slip into my inner landscape with ease.

The experience of depicting Brambly Hedge is an exhausting one because I must cut myself off from the everyday world in order to reach it. The intensity of the concentration, the tunnel vision if you like, stays with me for about half an hour after I stop working; it's a difficult transition. Luckily my husband and children are very patient and considerate with me and I have excellent support at home.

Has the success of the Brambly Hedge books made a great difference to your life?

It has brought advantages and disadvantages and, like Lord Woodmouse, I can't enjoy the one without the

other. There is a great deal of paperwork now, and because of the Brambly Hedge merchandise, a certain amount of consultation with the various manufacturers. I receive many letters from all over the world and I like to reply personally to all of them, though this can sometimes be difficult if I am in the middle of a book.

Children write and tell me which story they like best and give me suggestions for new books. Everyone seems to be waiting for Poppy to have some babies! Students want to know about my working methods and older people often write and tell me how much they'd like to live in Brambly Hedge, and how it reminds them of their childhood and a vanished way of life.

I am pleased that I receive as many letters from boys as girls. I like to know that they respond to a gentler kind of book – more than is generally supposed. And of course it is always exciting to receive letters from overseas. Producing books is a lonely way of life and I find these letters touching and encouraging.

However, in spite of all the excitements and new opportunities, at the end of the day I still like the things I have always liked: the country, looking after my garden, cooking, and spending time with my family.

For the last twelve years you have concentrated entirely on Brambly Hedge. Will you continue to do so?

The honest answer must be that I don't know! Now that I have a family of my own, I am even more committed to showing children a loving environment where everyone is valued and where the earth itself is appreciated and respected. All the things I want to say can so easily be incorporated into books about Brambly Hedge that there seems no good reason for change. I feel I have a duty to share my vision and to do it to the best of my ability, though each book is such a demanding task and I am never satisfied with the finished result because, sad to say, it never matches up to the picture in my mind.

JILL BARKLEM
JANE FIOR

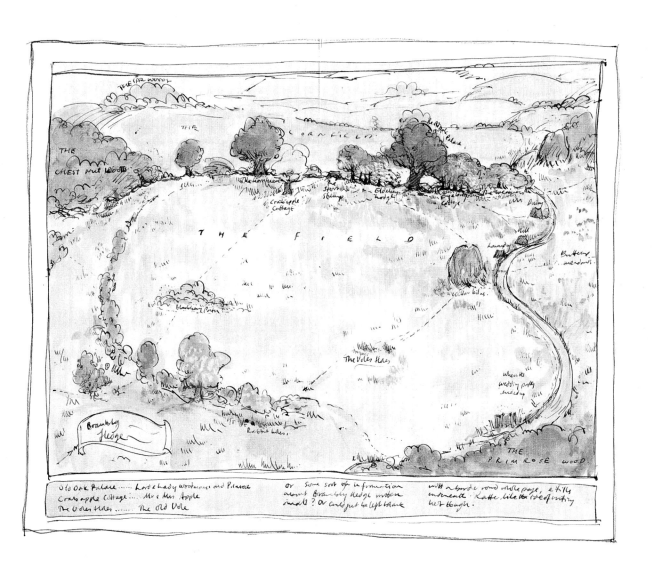

SPRING STORY

It was the most beautiful morning. The spring sunshine crept into every cottage along Brambly Hedge, and the little windows in the trees were opened wide.

All the mice were up early, but earliest of all was Wilfred, who lived with his family in the hornbeam tree. It was Wilfred's birthday.

Jumping out of bed, he ran into his parents' room, and bounced on their bed till they gave him their presents.

"Happy birthday, Wilfred," said Mr. and Mrs. Toadflax sleepily.

He tore off the pretty wrappings, and scattered them all over the floor. His squeaks of excitement woke his brother and sisters.

His parents turned over to go to sleep again. Wilfred went and sat on the stairs and blew his new whistle.

Mr. and Mrs. Apple lived next door at
Crabapple Cottage. The sound of Wilfred's
whistle floated in through their bedroom window.
Mrs. Apple got up and stretched. She sniffed the
sweet air and went down to the kitchen to make
a pot of elderflower tea. She was a very kindly
mouse and a wonderful cook. The cottage
always smelled of newly-made bread, fresh cakes
and blackberry puddings.

"Breakfast's ready," she called. Mr. Apple got
out of bed with a sigh, and joined her at the
kitchen table. They ate their toast and jam, and
listened to Wilfred's warbling.

"I think somebody needs a lesson from the
blackbird," said Mr. Apple, brushing the crumbs
from his whiskers and putting on his coat.
Mr. Apple was a nice, old-fashioned sort of
mouse. He was warden of the Store Stump where
all the food for Brambly Hedge was kept.

The Store Stump was not far away. As Mr.
Apple walked happily through the grass to the
big front doors, he felt someone pull his tail.
He turned around quickly. It was Wilfred,
whistle in hand.

"It's my birthday!" he squeaked.

"Is it, young mouse," said Mr. Apple. "Happy birthday to you! Would you like to come and help me check the Store Stump? We'll see what we can find."

In the middle of the Stump was an enormous hall, and leading off from it many passages and staircases. These led in turn to dozens of storerooms full of nuts and honey and jams and pickles. Each one had to be inspected. Wilfred's legs felt tired by the time they had finished, and he sat by the fire in the hall to rest. Mr. Apple lifted down a jar of sugared violets. He made a little cornet from a twist of paper, and filled it with sweets. Taking Wilfred by the paw, he led him through the dark corridors out into the sun. Wilfred went to look for his brother, and Mr. Apple hurried down the hedge to visit his daughter Daisy and her husband, Lord Woodmouse.

Lord and Lady Woodmouse lived in the Old Oak Palace in the middle of the hedge. From the outside, the Palace looked like an ordinary oak tree, but inside the trunk was hollowed out to form a beautiful and many-roomed mansion.

At its heart was the grand ballroom. Polished doors led to magnificent kitchens, dining rooms, bedrooms, playrooms, spiral staircases and secret passages. Old Oak Palace had always been the home of the Woodmouse family.

Upstairs in the best bedroom, Lord and Lady
Woodmouse woke to bright sunshine.

"What a perfect day!" sighed Lady Daisy as
she nibbled a primrose biscuit. When they heard
that Daisy's father had come to call, they were
soon up and dressed and running down the
winding stairs to greet him.

They found him in the kitchen drinking mint tea with Mrs. Crustybread, the Palace cook. Daisy gave Mr. Apple a kiss and sat down beside him.

"Hello Papa," she said. "What brings you here so early?"

"I've just met little Wilfred—it's his birthday today. Shall we arrange a surprise picnic for him?"

"What a wonderful idea," said Lord Woodmouse. Daisy nodded.

"I'll make him a special birthday cake if his mother agrees," said Mrs. Crustybread, hurrying off to the pantry to find the ingredients.

Everyone was to be invited of course, so Mr. Apple set off up the hedge towards the woods, and Lord Woodmouse went down towards the stream calling at each house on the way.

The first house on Mr. Apple's route was Elderberry Lodge. This fine elder bush was Basil's home. Basil was in charge of the Store Stump cellars. He was just getting up.

"A picnic eh? Splendid! I'll bring up some rose petal wine," he said, shuffling absent-mindedly round the room looking for his trousers. Basil had long white whiskers and always wore a scarlet waistcoat. He used to keep the other mice amused for hours with his stories.

"Ah, there you are, you rascals," he exclaimed, discovering his trousers behind the sofa.

Next Mr. Apple came to the hornbeam.
Mr. Toadflax was sitting on his front doorstep
eating bread and bramble jelly.

"We thought it would be nice to have a
surprise picnic for your Wilfred," whispered
Mr. Apple. "We won't tell him what it's for,
and we'll all meet at midday by the Palace roots."

Mr. Toadflax was delighted with the suggestion,
and went inside to tell his wife. Mr. Apple went
on to visit Old Vole who lived in a tussock of
grass in the middle of the field.

Lord Woodmouse, meanwhile, was working his way down to the stream. The news had travelled ahead of him, and all along the hedge excited mice leaned out of their windows to ask when the picnic would take place.

"I'll see if I can find some preserves," said old Mrs. Eyebright.

"Shall we bring tablecloths?" called the weavers who lived in the tangly hawthorn trees.

Poppy Eyebright from the dairy promised cheeses, and Dusty Dogwood, the Miller, offered a batch of buns.

Mice soon began calling at the Store Stump to collect clover flour and honey, bramble brandy and poppy seeds, and all the other good things needed for the picnic. Mrs. Crustybread baked a huge hazelnut cake with layers of thick cream, and Wilfred's mother decorated it. Mrs. Apple made some of her special primrose puddings.

Wilfred knew that there was to be an outing, and that if he behaved, he would be allowed to go. He did his best but with a new whistle, a drum and a peashooter for his birthday, it wasn't easy.

When the Toadflax family arrived at the Palace, Wilfred was rather disappointed that no one there seemed to know that it was his birthday. Indeed he had rather hoped for a few more presents, but

it would have been rude to drop hints, so he
hid his feelings as best he could. At a signal
from Lord Woodmouse they all set off with
their baskets, hampers and wheelbarrows.

Everyone had something to carry, Wilfred was
given an enormous basket, so heavy he could
hardly lift it. Mr. Apple lent him a wheelbarrow,
and his brother and sisters helped him to push it,
but still poor Wilfred found it hard to keep up.

It was a very long way. Heaving and pulling,
wheeling and hauling, the mice made their way
round the Palace, through the cornfield and
up by the stream. Wilfred felt very hot and he
wanted a rest.

"Here we are!" cried Lord Woodmouse at last.
The baskets were put down and opened,
and nettlestem cloths spread out on the mossy
grass. In no time at all, the food was unpacked.
Wilfred was exhausted. He sat on his basket,
too tired to open it, his whiskers drooping sadly.

Mr. Apple said grace: "For this good food from our green fields, may we be very grateful."

"I think the knives are in your basket, Wilfred," said Mrs. Apple kindly. "If you get them out, we can cut the pies."

Slowly, Wilfred slipped from his perch and undid the catch. When he lifted the lid, he could hardly believe his eyes.

Inside the hamper, packed all around with presents, was an enormous cake, and on the top, written in pink icing, was HAPPY BIRTHDAY WILFRED.

"*Happy Birthday, dear Wilfred,*
Happy Birthday to you," sang the mice.

When Wilfred had opened all his presents,
Basil said, "Give us a tune," so he bashfully
stood up and played *Hickory, Dickory, Dandelion
Clock* on his new whistle. Mrs. Toadflax nudged
him meaningfully when he had finished.

"Er . . . thank you for all my lovely presents,"
said Wilfred, trying to avoid Mrs. Crustybread's
eye. She had caught him firing acorns through
her kitchen window earlier in the day.

"Now for tea," announced Daisy Woodmouse. The mice sat on the grass and Wilfred handed round the cake.

When tea was over, the grown-ups snoozed under the bluebells, while the young mice played hide-and-seek in the primroses.

At last the sun began to sink behind the Far
Woods, and a chilly breeze blew over the field.
It was time to go home.

When the moon came up that night, Brambly
Hedge was silent and still. Every mouse was
fast asleep.

SUMMER STORY

It was a very hot summer.

Each day the sun rose high in the blue sky, and the fields shimmered in the heat.

The hedgerow was quiet. Many of the mice preferred to stay inside their shady cottages,

trying to keep cool.

Out of doors, the best place to be was down by the stream. The mice gathered there in the afternoon, sat under the bank in the shade, and dangled their paws and tails in the clear water.

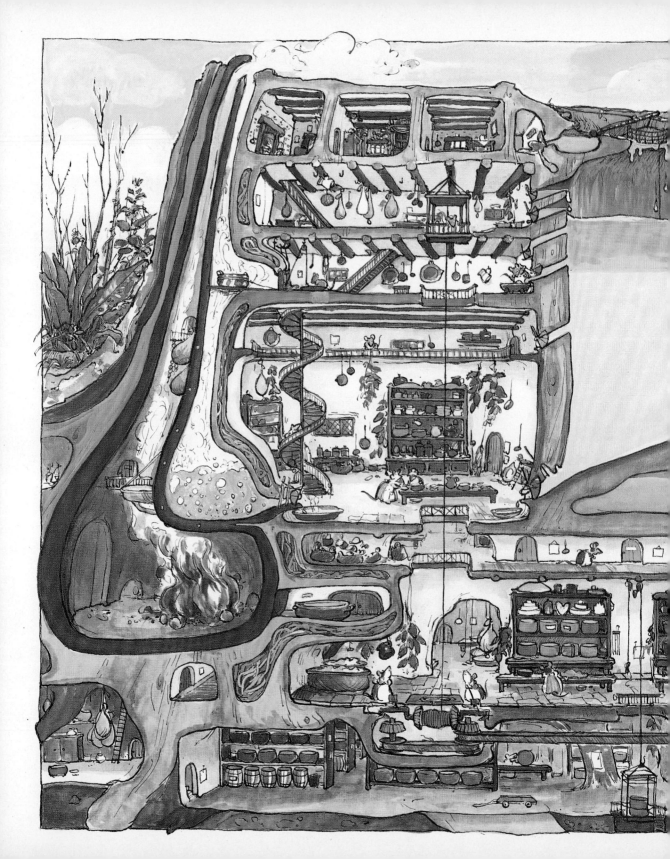

On the banks of the stream were the flour and dairy mills. The flow of the water turned the wheels which ground the flour and churned the butter for Brambly Hedge.

Poppy Eyebright looked after the Dairy Stump. She supervised the large vat into which milk, kindly given by some friendly cows, was poured and stored. The many kitchens, where cheeses were drained and shaped, smoked and wrapped, were also in her care.

Poppy was not fond of hot weather. Her pats of butter began to melt unless they were wrapped in cool dock leaves, and the pots of cream had to be hung in the millpool to keep them fresh.

When her work was finished she would wander out by the millwheel, enjoying the splashes of cool water.

The flour mill, further down the stream, was run by the miller, Dusty Dogwood. Dogwood was his family name, but he was called Dusty because he was always covered from tail to whiskers with flour dust.

He was a cheerful and friendly mouse,
like his father, his grandfather, and his great-
grandfather, who had all run the mill before him.
He loved the fine weather, and strolled up and
down the stream, chatting to the paddlers and
dabblers.

His walks took him past the Dairy, where
he would often see Poppy standing by the stream,
looking very pretty. As the long, hot days went by,
Dusty used to spend more and more time
walking up to the Dairy, and Poppy used to go
out more and more often to the mossy shadows
of the millwheel . . . .

Early in June, Miss Poppy Eyebright and Mr. Dusty Dogwood officially announced their engagement. Everyone along the hedgerow was delighted.

Midsummer's Day was picked for the wedding, and preparations were started at once. Poppy was so sure the weather would hold that they decided that the wedding should take place on the stream. It was the coolest place, and besides, it was very romantic.

Dusty found a large, flat piece of bark up in the woods, which a party of mice carried down to the water's edge. It was floated, with some difficulty, just under the mill weir, and tethered in midstream by plaited rush and nettle ropes.

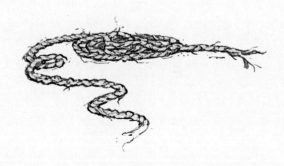

Poppy prepared her trousseau. Every afternoon, she sat in the shade of some tall kingcups embroidering her wedding dress, which she hid as soon as she saw anyone coming along the path.

The wedding day dawned at last. The sky
was clear and blue, and it was hotter than ever.
The kitchens of Brambly Hedge were full of
activity. Cool summer foods were being made.
There was cold watercress soup, fresh dandelion
salad, honey creams, syllabubs and meringues.

The young mice had been up early to gather
huge baskets of wild strawberries.

Basil selected some white wines, primrose,
meadowsweet and elderflower, and hung them to
cool in the rushes. Basil was in charge of all the
cellars under the Store Stump. He was a stout,
good-natured mouse, with long white whiskers,
and a sensitive nose for fine wine.

In her rooms above the Dairy, Poppy dressed carefully. She polished her whiskers, and dabbed rosewater behind her ears. Her straw bonnet, which Lady Woodmouse had trimmed with flowers, hung from the bedpost, and her bridal posy lay waiting on the windowsill. She peeped at her reflection in the shiny wardrobe door, took a deep breath, and ran downstairs to join her bridesmaids.

Dusty kept his best suit in a basket under the stairs to protect it from the moths. He put it on, and tucked a daisy in his buttonhole.

"I'd better just check that barley I ground yesterday," he said to himself. He ran up the steps at such a pace that the whole mill seemed to shake. The wooden floor above him let down a cloud of dust, all over his new wedding suit.

"Bother it!" he said, sitting on a sack of corn, and looking at his mottled jacket in dismay.

There was a thumping on the door below, and his friend Conker called through the letterbox,

"Dusty, are you ready? It's nearly time to go."

Dusty sighed, and went morosely down the stairs.

As soon as Conker saw him, he began to giggle.

"Dusty by name, dusty by nature," he said, trying to remedy matters with his clean handkerchief.

The flour dust swirled, and settled again on whiskers, tails, best clothes and buttonholes. The two mice looked at each other, and started to laugh. They laughed so much that they had to sit down on a flour bag to recover.

The wedding was to take place at midday, and Dusty and Conker arrived just in time. The guests were all in their finest clothes. Three young mice, dressed in smart blue suits, had been chosen as pages, and were busily directing everyone to their places. Mrs. Apple discreetly tried to dust down the groom and best man, but to little avail.

At last old Mrs. Eyebright, Poppy's grandmother, spotted the bride and her little bridesmaids coming through the grass. The pages squeaked with excitement, and got into place. Every head turned to watch the bride as she made her way through the buttercups and stepped onto the decorated raft.

The Old Vole, who had been asked to perform the ceremony, stood up, and said in a kindly voice: "Poppy Eyebright, do you love Dusty Dogwood, and will you love him and care for him

for ever and ever?" Poppy vowed that she would.
"Dusty Dogwood, do you love Poppy, and will
you love her and look after her for ever and ever?"
"I will," said Dusty. Mrs. Apple blew her nose.

"Then in the name of the flowers and the fields, the stars in the sky, and the streams that flow down to the sea, and the mystery that breathes wonder into all these things, I pronounce you mouse and wife."

All the mice cheered as Dusty kissed his bride, and the bridesmaids threw baskets of petals over the happy couple. Mrs. Apple wiped a tear from her eye, and the dancing and feasting began.

First they danced, for no one could keep still, jigs, reels and quadrilles.

Mr. Apple proposed a toast.

"To the bride and groom! May their tails grow long, and their eyes be bright, and all their squeaks be little ones."

The guests raised their glasses, and then they danced again. The dancing was so vigorous that the raft bobbed up and down. Gradually the ropes holding the raft began to wear through.

One by one, the little ropes snapped, until finally the very last one gave way.

They were carried into midstream by the
current. The young mice squeaked with alarm at
first, but as they seemed to come to no harm, they
continued with the feast.

The raft floated gently past fields of buttercups and meadowsweet, and the voles tending the fires in the Pottery came out to wave as the wedding party drifted by.

Eventually, the raft was caught in a leafy clump of rushes and forget-me-nots. The ropes were made fast, and the dancing began again.

At last the dusk came, golden and misty over the
fields. The blue sky slowly darkened, and the mice
began to think about getting home. All the food
was finished up, and the pots and pans hidden in
the rushes to be collected the next day.

They walked back through the fields in the
evening sun, looking very splendid in their
wedding clothes. The Old Vole was taken back to
his hole first, and the rest of the mice gradually
made their way home to bed, exhausted but happy.

And what happened to Poppy and Dusty?

They slipped quietly away to the primrose woods. The primroses were over, but there, hidden amongst the long grass and ferns, wild roses and honeysuckle, was the cottage in which they had chosen to stay.

It was the perfect place for a honeymoon.

AUTUMN STORY

It was a fine autumn. The blackberries were ripe, and the nuts were ready, and the mice of Brambly Hedge were very busy. Every morning they went out into the fields to gather seeds, berries and roots, which they took back to the Store Stump, and carefully stowed away for the winter ahead. The Store Stump was warm inside, and smelled deliciously of bramble jelly and rising bread, and it was already nearly full of food.

Lord Woodmouse, who lived in the Old Oak Palace, was out early with his youngest daughter, Primrose.

"Now keep close to me, and don't get lost," he said, as they made their way along the blackberry bushes. Primrose picked the berries nearest the ground while her father hooked the upper branches down with his walking stick.

The basket was nearly full when they were joined by old Mrs. Eyebright.

"I've been looking for you," she said. "Bad weather's on its way, I can feel it in my bones. We must finish our harvesting before the rain begins."

Lord Woodmouse sent Primrose back to the Palace, and then went on to the Store Stump to find Mr. Apple to make arrangements. Soon parties of mice with carts and wheelbarrows were hurrying out to the fields to gather the last of the nuts and berries.

Lord and Lady Woodmouse decided to help pick mushrooms, and they were just setting off when Lady Woodmouse cried out in alarm, "Where's Primrose?"

She was nowhere to be seen.

She wasn't hiding in the baskets, or under the leaves, or in the long grass.

"Has anyone seen Primrose?" shouted Lord Woodmouse.

"She hasn't been here," replied the mice gathering berries high in the blackthorn bush.

"We haven't seen her," called the mice in the tangly hawthorn trees.

The children thought she was at her grandmother's house, and a search party was sent along to investigate.

Hot and out of breath, they knocked at the door of Crabapple Cottage.

"Have you seen Primrose?" asked Wilfred. "We've lost her."

Mrs. Apple shook her head, took off her apron, and joined in the search. Mr. Apple ran over to the gap in the hedge by the Store Stump.

"Primrose, where are you?" he cried.

"Primrose, where are you?" echoed the call across the cornfield.

Lord and Lady Woodmouse went back to the
Palace. They looked in the cupboards, and under
the beds. The Store Stump was searched from
top to bottom.

"Oh dear!" said Lady Daisy. "She's such a
little mouse. Where can she be? What shall
we do?"

Meanwhile, Primrose, wandering along the edge of the cornfield, was quite unaware of her parent's concern. She had spent the morning picking wild flowers and gazing up at the blue sky, and after a lunch of blackberries, she had dozed a little in the sun. She was just going to help a group of mice she had seen gathering seeds in the ditch, when she spotted a little round house high up in the stalks of the corn.

"I wonder who lives there," she thought, and decided to climb up and peep through one of the windows.

As she looked in, she saw two pairs of bright little eyes peering back at her.

"I – I do beg your pardon," she stammered, and began to climb down again.

"We were just going to have tea," a voice called after her, "Won't you join us?"

Primrose found the tiny front door, and went inside. It was very cosy. There was a thistledown carpet on the floor, and the neatly-woven grass walls were covered with books and pictures. The two elderly harvest mice who lived in the house were very glad to have a visitor. They sat Primrose down, gave her a slice of cake, and handed her their album of family portraits to look at.

When Primrose had been shown all their treasures, she thanked the mice politely, and climbed down to the ground again. She decided to walk to the edge of the Chestnut Woods before she went home. Some Brambly Hedge mice were still there, picking blackberries in the last of the evening sun, but they were too busy to notice her. She peered into the grasses, looking for feathers and other useful things.

Hidden in the brambles, she discovered a very interesting hole.

"I wonder if anyone lives down there," she said to herself, and wandered into the tunnel.

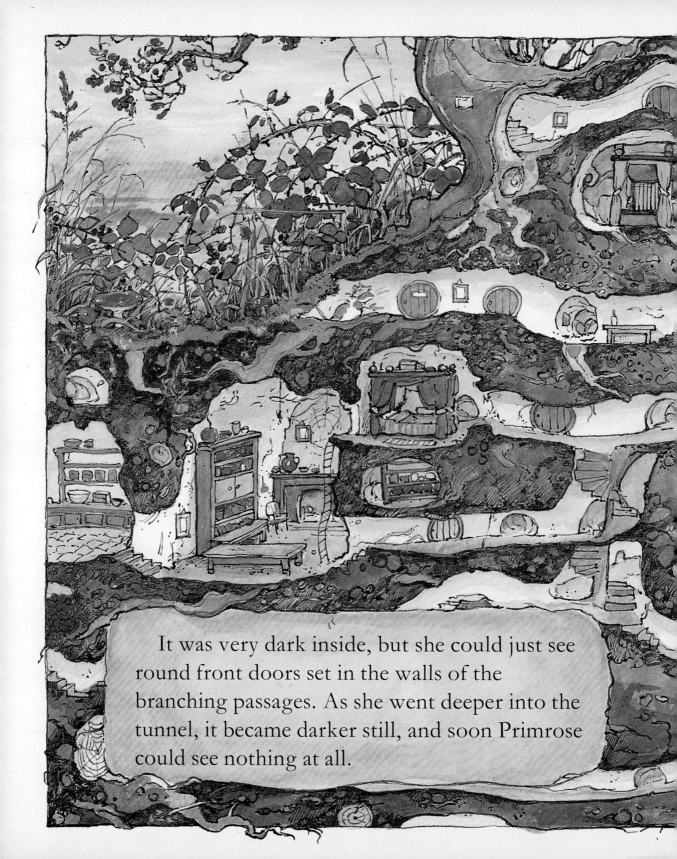

It was very dark inside, but she could just see round front doors set in the walls of the branching passages. As she went deeper into the tunnel, it became darker still, and soon Primrose could see nothing at all.

"I don't think I like this place," said Primrose
with a shiver, "I'm going home."

She turned to leave, but with so many
passages leading this way and that, she had no
idea which way she had come. She picked up
her skirts, and ran through the maze of tunnels.

At last she saw a glimmer of light, and ran towards it. The passage opened into a thick clump of brambles and briars under some tall trees. Primrose had no idea where she was.

"I can't see the oak tree," she said in a small voice, "and I can't see the willow by the stream. I think I must be lost."

It was getting very dark. Big drops of rain began to fall, and splashed through the leaves around her. Primrose huddled under a toadstool, and tried not to cry.

In the distance a lonely owl hooted, and the branches of the trees above creaked in the rising wind. There were little scrabbling noises in the bush quite near to Primrose, and these worried her most of all.

It got darker and darker, and soon everything disappeared into the night.

Primrose was just trying not to think about weasels, when to her horror she saw five little flickering lights coming through the woods towards her. She could just make out five strange

figures behind them. They were shapeless and
bulgy, and seemed to have no heads at all.
Primrose wriggled further back into the brambles.

The figures came closer and closer, and
Primrose realised that they were going to pass
right by her hiding place.

The nearer they came, the worse they looked, and she shut her eyes as she heard them pass only a whisker away from where she was sitting. One . . . two . . . three . . . four . . . .

She decided to be very brave and take a peep
at the fifth as it went by.

It walked with a limp. It had a tail. And
whiskers. And Mr. Apple's trousers.

"GRANDPA!" she squeaked with delight.

As each of the figures turned round she recognised them; Mr. Apple, Mrs. Apple, Dusty Dogwood, and best of all, her own mother and father.

Primrose pushed her way through the brambles.

"Primrose!" cried Lady Daisy. "You're safe!"

"The harvest mice said you had gone to the woods, but it was so dark and wet that we'd almost given up hope of finding you," said her father, and picked her up and wrapped her snugly in his cloak.

Primrose was nearly asleep by the time they got home. Lady Woodmouse carried her up to her little room, and took off her wet clothes. A clean nightie was warming by the fire, and a mug of hot acorn coffee had been placed by the bed.

"I'll never ever go out of the field on my own again," Primrose whispered sleepily.

Her mother gave her a kiss, and smoothed her pillow.

"*Ease your whiskers, rest your paws,*
   Pies and puddings fill the stores.
   Sweetly dream the night away,
   Till sunshine brings another day,"
. . . she sang softly, tucking Primrose into her comfy bed.

WINTER STORY

It was the middle of winter. The sun had just set, and it was very, very cold. An icy wind was blowing from the East, and the wind promised snow.

Deep in the dark roots of Brambly Hedge tiny lights appeared as lamps were lit in the windows.

More little lights could be seen leaving the Store Stump, moving hastily along the hedgerow, and disappearing into holes hidden in the twisty roots. The mice had smelled snow in the air, and were all hurrying home to a nice hot supper by the fire.

Mr. Apple, warden of the Store Stump, was the last to leave for home. By the time he reached Crabapple Cottage, the first flakes were beginning to fall.

"Is that you, dear?" called Mrs. Apple as he let himself in through the front door. Delicious smells wafted down from the kitchen. Mrs. Apple had spent the afternoon baking pies, cakes and puddings for the cold days to come. She drew two armchairs up to the fire, and brought in their supper on a tray.

There was a lot of noise coming from the
hornbeam tree next door. The Toadflax children
had never seen snow before.

"It's snowing! It really is SNOWING!"
squeaked the two boys, Wilfred and Teasel. They

chased their sisters Clover and Catkin round the kitchen, with pawfuls of snow scooped from the windowsill.

"Suppertime!" called Mrs. Toadflax firmly, ladling hot chestnut soup into four small bowls.

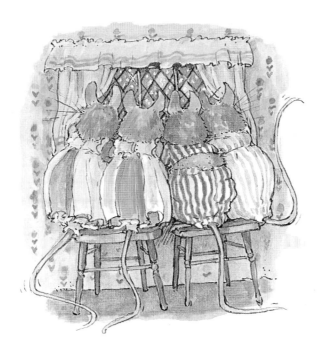

After supper the children were sent off to bed, but they were far too excited to sleep. As soon as the grown-ups were safely occupied downstairs, they climbed out of their bunk beds to watch the snowflakes falling past the window.

"Tobogganing tomorrow," said Wilfred.

"Snow pancakes for tea," said Clover.

"We'll make a snow mouse," said Catkin.

"And I'll knock it down!" said Teasel, pushing the girls off their chair.

Next morning the mice along the hedgerow
woke to find their windows half-blocked by snow.
Mrs. Apple had to stand on tiptoes on the
kitchen table to see out. And what a sight met

her eyes! The fields were covered with a thick, white blanket of snow, and all the paths and plants had disappeared beneath it.

When the Toadflax family went down to breakfast, they found the kitchen dark and still. Mrs. Toadflax put fresh wood on the fire, and set Clover to work with the toasting fork. Soon they were all sitting round the table, eating hot buttered toast, drinking blackberry leaf tea, and making plans for the day ahead.

The snow was thicker than the mice had expected. All the downstairs windows along the hedgerow were covered with snow, and many of the upper ones, too, were hidden in deep drifts.

The mice leaned out of their bedroom windows to wave and call to their friends.

"Enough for a Snow Ball, wouldn't you say?" called Toadflax to Mrs. Apple.

"A Snow Ball!" echoed the little mice, gleefully.

Every family along the hedgerow kept shovels, maps and ropes in a special cupboard by the front door, and after breakfast the mice dug tunnels from tree to tree, linking them all to the Store Stump. Teasel and Wilfred were sent down to help, but they soon found that it was much more fun to throw snow at each other, and so were sent home again.

Lord Woodmouse dug his way through to
old Mrs. Eyebright, and helped her to light
a fire.

"I haven't seen snow like this since I was
young," she sighed. "The last Snow Ball was
held in the year Mr. Eyebright and I were
married. I'm the only one left who can remember
it now."

When the tunnels were finished, all the mice
gathered noisily in the Store Stump Hall.

Mrs. Apple took some seed cake from the cupboard, and prepared a jug of acorn coffee. The mice helped themselves, and gathered round Mr. Apple, who held up a paw for silence.

"Lord Woodmouse and I have agreed," he said when they were quiet, "that we should follow in the tradition of our forefathers." He cleared his throat nervously, straightened his whiskers, and recited,

> *"When the snows are lying deep,*
> *When the field has gone to sleep,*
> *When the blackthorn turns to white,*
> *And frosty stars bejewel the night,*
> *When summer streams are turned to ice,*
> *A Snow Ball warms the hearts of mice.*

"Friends, I declare that a Snow Ball will take place at dusk tonight in the Ice Hall."

"Where's that?" whispered Clover, as the mice clapped and cheered.

"Wait and see!" replied Mrs. Apple. "You come home with me and help prepare the feast."

There was a deep drift of snow banked against the Store Stump, and the elder mice, after discussion, declared it to be "just right" for the Ice Hall. Mr. Apple dug the first tunnel to check that the snow was firm.

"It's perfect!" he called back from the middle of the drift. The mice picked up their shovels, and the digging began.

The snow was dug from inside the drift, piled into carts, and taken down to the stream. Wilfred and Teasel helped enthusiastically, but they were sent home again when Mr. Apple caught them putting icicles down Catkin's dress.

The middle of the drift was carefully hollowed out. Mr. Apple inspected the roof very thoroughly to make sure that it was safe.

"Safe as the Store Stump!" he declared.

All the kitchens along Brambly Hedge were
warm and busy. Hot soups, punches and puddings
bubbled, and in the ovens pies browned and sizzled.
Clover and Catkin helped Mrs. Apple string

crabapples to roast over the fire. The boys had to
sit and watch because they ate too many.

"It's not that I mind, dears, but we must have
SOME left for the punch!"

The Glow-worms were put in charge of the lighting. Toadflax fetched them early from the bank at the end of the Hedge, for Mrs. Apple had insisted that they should have a good supper before their long night's work began.

By tea-time the Hall was finished. The ice columns and carvings sparkled in the blue-green light, and the polished dance floor shone. Tables were set at the end of the Hall, and eager cooks bustled in from their kitchens with baskets of food.

The children decorated a small raised platform with sprays of holly, while Basil, the keeper of the hedgerow wines, set out some chairs for the musicians.

When all was done, the mice admired their handiwork, and went home to wash and change.

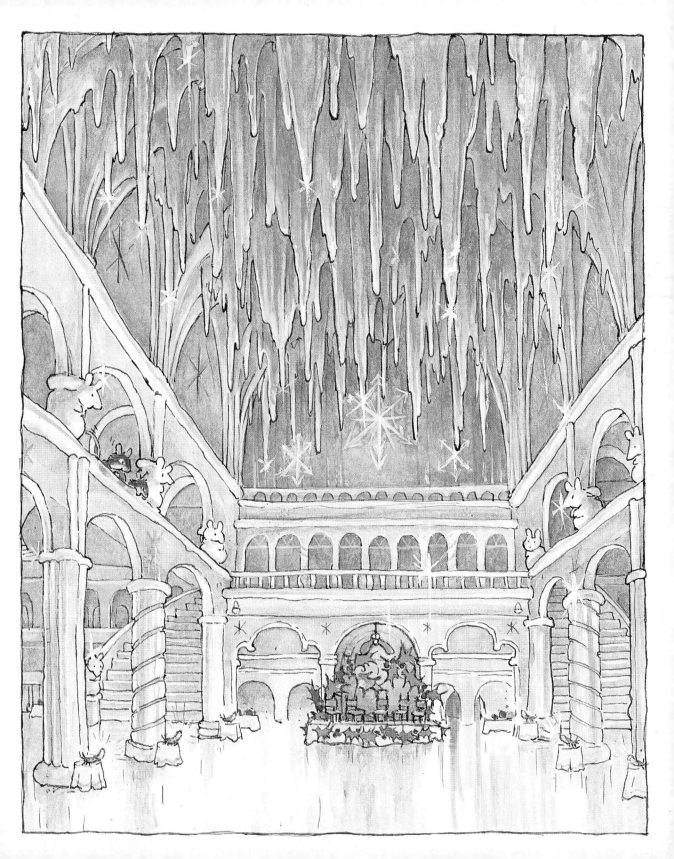

As muffs and mufflers were left at the door, it
was clear that all the mice had dressed up for the
grand occasion. Wilfred and Teasel crept under
a table to watch, and every now and then a little
paw appeared and a cream cake disappeared.

Basil struck up a jolly tune on his violin, and
the dancing began. All the dances were very fast

and twirly, and were made even faster by the
slippery ice floor. Wilfred and Teasel whirled
their sisters round so quickly that their paws left
the ground.

"I don't feel very well," said Clover, looking
rather green.

Mrs. Apple stood on a chair, and banged two saucepan lids together.

"Supper is served," she called.

The eating and drinking and dancing carried
on late into the night. At midnight, all the
hedgerow children were taken home to bed.

As soon as they were safely tucked up, their parents returned to the Ball. Basil made some hot blackberry punch, and the dancing got faster and faster.

The Snow Ball went on until dawn.

The musicians were tired. The ice columns began to drip. The sleepy mice could dance no more. They wandered home through the snow tunnels, climbed the stairs, and crept into their warm beds.

Outside the windows, the snow had started to fall again.

But every mouse in Brambly Hedge was fast asleep.